A NO RULE DAY

Author
ANNA PAYNE GLASS
Illustrator
T.J PAYNE

Print information available on the last page

Rev. date: 10/13/2015

To order additional copies of this book, contact:
Xlibris
1-888-795-4274
www.Xlibris.com
Orders@Xlibris.com

A NO RULE DAY

"It's bedtime", said Mom.
Amy said," I hate bedtime!
I wish there were no more
rules!" "Ok", said Mom.
"There are no more rules.
You can go to bed when
ever you want."

Amy fell asleep on the floor.
Mom carried her to bed.

The next morning at breakfast
Amy pushed away. " I don't
want anything", she said.
"ok. No rules about
breakfast" Mom said,
As she took the food away.

On the way to school Amy was hungry. She wished her mom had made her eat.

Amy screamed as her Mom ran a STOP sign. "Didn't you see that sign and the car that almost hit us?!" "No rules", Mom said.

When Amy went into class, her friend, Jamaal was on the floor crying. He had fallen off the table. There was no rule about not climbing on the furniture any more.

14

Yolanda and Tamika were fighting in housekeeping and the teacher just watched.

Amy wanted to work a puzzle but all the pieces were mixed together. The whole room was a mess, and very noisy.

Amy asked, "When is lunch? I am hungry!" "Whenever they want to bring it". Replied the teacher. "We have no rule about lunch time."

"I want the rules back", Amy screamed, waking herself up. She was glad to find that it has only been a dream.

Mom came in to kiss her good morning. "Ready for breakfast?" she asked. "Yes, said Amy, and all the rules

Printed in the United States
by Baker & Taylor Publisher Services